Mrs Pepperpot's
and other sto

As Mr Pepperpot passed the place where he had spilt the first ice-cream, he made the mistake of looking down. And do you know? The ice-cream on the ground was *moving*! Poor Mr Pepperpot dropped the second cornet on the first one and fled back to the kiosk. He was sure there was a snake in the grass, and he was very much afraid of snakes.

And what was going on down there in the grass where two double ice-creams were bubbling and churning like porridge on the boil? You've guessed it. Mrs Pepperpot was underneath! She had got out of the car to stretch her legs, and then, suddenly, she had SHRUNK to the size of a pepperpot!

Also in Beaver by Alf Prøysen

Little Old Mrs Pepperpot

Mrs Pepperpot Again

Alf Prøysen

MRS PEPPERPOT'S OUTING

Translated by Marianne Helweg

Illustrated by Bjorn Berg

Beaver Books

A Beaver Book

Published by Arrow Books Limited
62-65 Chandos Place, London WC2N 4NW

An imprint of Century Hutchinson Ltd

London Melbourne Sydney Auckland
Johannesburg and agencies throughout
the world

First published by Hutchinson Children's Books 1971
Beaver edition 1988
Reprinted 1988

Printed and bound in Great Britain by
The Guernsey Press Co. Ltd,
Guernsey, Channel Islands.

ISBN 0 09 957410 1

Contents

Mrs Pepperpot's Outing

I

It was a beautiful sunny summer morning, and Mrs Pepperpot was standing at her kitchen window peeling onions. You remember Mrs Pepperpot? She's the little old woman who lives on a hillside in Norway and has the habit of shrinking to the size of a pepperpot at the most inconvenient moments.

Well, here she was, peeling onions, and from time to time she sniffed a little, the way people do when they are peeling onions. As the tears rolled down her cheeks she wiped them away with the back of her hand and sighed. She was not feeling very happy.

But Mr Pepperpot was; he was on holiday. Now he came rushing through the door with his hat askew, and his hair all over the place. Waving his arms, he shouted: 'I've good news for you, Mrs P! Guess what it is.'

'Good news?' said Mrs Pepperpot. 'Have you found me a new pet?' Because she had just been thinking how empty and sad the house was without even a cat or a dog.

'No, no, something *much* better. You'll have to have another guess,' said her husband. 'Pets! How can you be so old-fashioned? They're a dead loss when you want to go away anywhere, always needing to be fed and looked after.'

'But I *like* looking after animals; they're fun,' she answered. 'Besides, quite often one doesn't really *want* to go away, and then it's very useful to be able to say you have to look after the animals.' She wiped away another tear: 'Oh, those onions!'

'Well, I think you're behind the times,' said Mr Pepperpot. 'It's good for everyone to get about and not be stuck in one place all your life.'

This made Mrs Pepperpot laugh. 'Did you say get about? How far do we get in your old wreck of a car? The person who's stuck in one place is *you* with your head under the bonnet every night for weeks on end!'

'It's my hobby,' said Mr Pepperpot. 'Everyone should have a hobby nowadays. It says in the paper you should make good use of your free time.'

You see, Mr Pepperpot had bought an old car cheaply, and ever since he had been tinkering with it, putting in new parts and cleaning and polishing it.

'You still haven't guessed my news, so I'll tell you,' he said. 'We're going for an outing in the car!'

'You mean you've really got it working?' Mrs Pepperpot could hardly believe it. 'Where are we going?'

'There's a car rally over the other side of Blocksberg: it's for old cars, so I thought I might enter mine. I might even win a cup.'

This was a sore point with Mr Pepperpot. His wife knew

he had always wanted to win a cup or a trophy. They did have one in the house, but she kept it hidden at the back of a cupboard, because it was one *she* had won when she was a young girl, and worked on a farm. She had got it for being so good at looking after the livestock. Now she would really like Mr Pepperpot to have one too, so she said:

'Yes, let's go. An outing would be fun, and we can take a picnic.'

'I'll just go and check the engine once more; be ready in half an hour.'

Mrs Pepperpot bustled about; she was quite looking forward to seeing some new places after the long winter at home. She got out the picnic basket, hard-boiled some

eggs, packed bread and butter and a piece of cold ham and some pancakes left over from last night. As she worked she made up a little song to sing in the car. This is how it went, to the tune of 'Nuts in May':

'My hubby is mad about motoring,
Motoring, motoring,
He spends his evenings tinkering
On his rickety automobile.

So now we'll be bouncing up and down
Up and down, up and down,
Everything in the back seat is thrown
Off the rickety automobile!

I may be crazy to go with him,
Go with him, go with him,
But oh, he's made it look so trim,
His rickety automobile!

At least we'll have a fine picnic,
A fine picnic, a fine picnic,
With sausages, bread and ham and chick
In his rickety automobile!

And then of course we'll see the sights,
See the sights, see the sights,
Of valleys and forests and mountain heights
From his rickety automobile!

Hooray!'

Mr Pepperpot grumbled when she brought the loaded basket out to the car. 'What do we want with all that stuff? Much better to buy ice-cream as we go along and there are plenty of cafés where we can have a hot-dog and ketchup.' He liked to show that he knew what tourists did when they went motoring.

'No nourishment in ice-cream,' said Mrs Pepperpot. 'And I don't trust cafés.' With that she dumped the basket in the back seat and got in.

Mr Pepperpot got in the driving seat. But just before he started the engine he had a sudden thought: 'You won't *shrink* while we're out, will you?'

'Oh, stop fussing!' said Mrs Pepperpot, as she settled herself comfortably. 'You know I never have any idea when it's going to happen. If it does, it does, and I usually manage, don't I? Start up, Mr P, I'm quite looking forward to this outing!'

So off they went. At first Mr Pepperpot drove very carefully down the little country road from the house. But once they were on the main road, with its smooth asphalt surface, he put his foot on the pedal and they hummed along at quite a good pace. He started to whistle; Mr Pepperpot always did that when he was happy.

'This is the life!' he sang. 'All these years I've been mucking about with an old horse and cart, never getting

anywhere, never seeing anything.'

'I don't know,' said Mrs Pepperpot. 'You used to get around quite well on a bicycle—fast enough to break your neck!'

'Yes, but think of the advantages of a motor-car: four wheels, comfortable seats, plenty of room for luggage and a roof to keep the rain out.'

'Plenty of expense too,' answered Mrs Pepperpot, 'and plenty of time needed for repairs. When will you ever get around to clearing the drains or help me dig up potatoes now?'

'Stop grumbling and enjoy yourself!' ordered Mr Pepperpot as he slowed down over a little bridge. On the other side there was a kiosk selling ice-cream.

'There, didn't I tell you we could get ice-cream?' said

Mr Pepperpot. 'I'll go and get you one.' So he hopped out of the car and went over to the kiosk to buy a double vanilla cornet for Mrs Pepperpot. 'That should put her in a good mood,' he said to himself, as he balanced his way back towards the car with it. But half-way there he was distracted by a hissing noise in the grass at his feet.

'Oops!' he said, and dropped the beautiful ice-cream!

There was nothing for it but to go back for another. He paid his money and the girl gave him a second ice-cream as big as the first. Back he went, holding the cornet with its great mound on top very steady. But as he passed the place where he had spilt the first one, he made the mistake of looking down. And do you know? The ice-

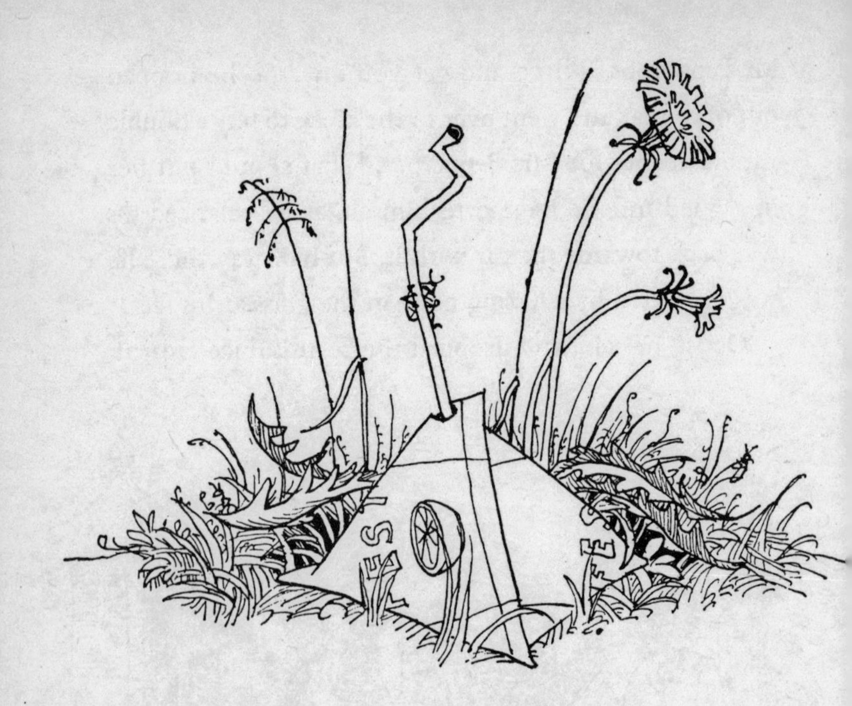

cream on the ground was *moving*! Poor Mr Pepperpot dropped the second cornet on the first one and fled back to the kiosk. He was sure there was a snake in the grass, and he was very much afraid of snakes.

But back at the kiosk a bus-load of trippers had just lined up for refreshments and Mr Pepperpot had to stand at the end of the queue.

And what was going on down there in the grass where two double ice-creams were bubbling and churning like porridge on the boil? You've guessed it: Mrs Pepperpot was underneath! She had got out of the car to stretch

her legs, and then, suddenly, she had SHRUNK to the size of a pepperpot!

There she was, right in Mr Pepperpot's path; she was so afraid he might step on her that she hissed like a snake, and the next thing she knew, she was struggling to get her head clear of a freezing cold and sticky mess! She had only just started breathing again when dollop! She was covered with another portion of ice-cream as big, cold and sticky as the first!

Poor Mrs Pepperpot didn't know what to do; she'd never be able to dig her way out alone. 'I'll just freeze to death,' she thought miserably. But after a little while she felt the load of ice-cream growing lighter, and soon she could push her head through.

'That's better!' she said.

'It's jolly good!' said a voice next to her, and there stood a young kitten, licking his chops and purring.

'What a beautiful, clever little pussy you are!' cried

Mrs Pepperpot, wiping the ice-cream from her face.

'Mm, can't say *you're* exactly beautiful, but you taste very good,' said the kitten. 'Are you made of ice-cream right through? I mean, will I be able to eat you all up?'

'Certainly not!' cried Mrs Pepperpot. 'Ice-cream right through indeed! What an idea! No, my friend, I'm just an ordinary woman most of the time. But now and then I shrink to this size. Come to think of it, I don't mind if you do lick me clean—help yourself!'

The kitten set to work very willingly. He was so thorough that soon Mrs Pepperpot had to shout to him to stop.

'I'm very ticklish, you see,' she said, laughing. 'Fancy me getting a cat-lick; I never expected that when we set off in the car this morning.'

'You have a car?' asked the kitten.

'My husband does; we're on an outing—or we were till this happened. Where do you live?'

The kitten hung his head: 'Nowhere, really. I did live in a barn with my mother, but some people came along and picked me up. They took me back to their house and gave me lots of food—that's where I got my taste for ice-cream. They used to play with me and at night they would tuck me up in a little basket. It was a wonderful life!'

'What happened then?'

'Well, they didn't belong in this place—they were just on holiday. So suddenly, yesterday, they packed up all their stuff, locked the door of the house and got in their car and drove off. I thought I was going too, of course, but they must have forgotten all about me, because they didn't even bother to look back or wave goodbye.'

'I see,' said Mrs Pepperpot, looking thoughtful. 'So now you have no home?'

'No,' said the kitten, 'there's no one to feed me or play with me or call me in at night. Until I found you and the ice-cream I hadn't had anything to eat since yesterday.' He licked the last bit of ice-cream out of Mrs Pepperpot's ear with the point of his rough tongue.

'It was just as well I did shrink today,' said Mrs Pepperpot. 'People like that shouldn't be allowed to keep pets.

Animals are not just playthings for children to throw away when they don't need them any more. Fancy going off and not even asking a neighbour to look after you!' Mrs Pepperpot was getting really worked up, as she always did when people were thoughtless or unkind to animals.

The kitten was watching her with his head on one side: 'Couldn't you take me home with you and let me be your pussy? You're fond of animals, aren't you? And you can talk cat language.'

'Well,' said Mrs Pepperpot, 'there are one or two snags. My husband is *not* very fond of animals, especially young kittens. And as to understanding cat language, I can only do that when I am small.'

'Will you grow large again soon?'

'I don't know.'

'Will I be afraid of you when you do?'

Mrs Pepperpot laughed. 'I shouldn't think so. But if you could manage to carry me on your back over to that old car there, I might grow to my normal size quite soon.'

'I'll try. Climb up!'

But though Mrs Pepperpot got on his back all right, she was too heavy for the kitten to carry.

'Perhaps I could pull you along by your skirt,' he suggested.

'I don't mind what you do,' said Mrs Pepperpot, as she lay down on the ground with her arms tucked under her head; 'pull away!'

The kitten took Mrs Pepperpot's skirt between his teeth and dragged her as carefully as he could down the path, trying to avoid the ice-cream puddle and empty cartons and drinking straws that people had dropped.

'I hope I'm not bumping you too much,' said the kitten.

'Not at all,' answered Mrs Pepperpot, 'I have a fine view of the sky overhead and the birds and the trees.'

But now we had better see what was happening to Mr Pepperpot. We left him in the queue and he stood there a long, long time before he got served again. This time he bought the biggest possible cornet and made

straight for the car, hoping Mrs Pepperpot had not lost patience with him altogether.

'Supposing she has shrunk and I won't be able to find her?' he thought anxiously, but when he opened the back door of the car, there she sat, as large as life.

'Oh my! Am I glad to see you!' He sighed with relief.

'You sound as if I'd been to the moon and back,' she said.

'Well, you see, if you had shrunk and disappeared, I'd never have got through all this ice-cream.' And he held out the cornet.

'Get along with you—I told you to stop fussing,' said Mrs Pepperpot. She set the cornet carefully into the corner of the basket.

'Aren't you going to eat it after all that?' Mr Pepperpot sounded a little hurt.

'All in good time. We'd better be getting on now, if you're going to enter for the rally.'

'I'm not sure I'll bother with that car rally,' he said. 'While I was standing in the queue at the kiosk I heard someone talking about a cross-country race, and it's not as far to drive as the car rally. Shall we go there instead?'

'It's all one to me,' said Mrs Pepperpot, 'as long as we're enjoying ourselves.'

Mr Pepperpot beamed. 'Yes, we are, aren't we?'

He didn't know that Mrs Pepperpot meant herself and the kitten, which was safely hidden in the basket and enjoying a good lick at that giant ice-cream.

II

The road was smooth and they were driving along quite comfortably when Mr Pepperpot suddenly stopped the car.

'Did you hear something?' he asked his wife.

She shook her head. They drove on a bit further, but then he stopped again.

'Didn't you hear anything this time?' he asked.

No, she didn't and he drove on again. But when he stopped for the third time Mr Pepperpot said: 'You must have heard it; it sounded just like a cat miaowing.'

'Probably your brakes have got wet,' suggested Mrs Pepperpot.

'I'll have a look,' said Mr Pepperpot, and got out.

Mrs Pepperpot stayed where she was and stroked the kitten to keep him quiet. After a while she asked her husband if he'd found anything; she knew you shouldn't rush a man when he's looking for trouble in his car.

'Not yet!' came the answer from under the bonnet.

'Perhaps the engine is overheated?'

'Yes, I think I'll get some water from that farm up on the hill.' He took out a green plastic bucket and started trudging up the hill. He could see there was a pump in the front yard.

The farm was quite a long way off, so Mrs Pepperpot thought she could safely take a short stroll with the kitten. The little creature was very good, running along

beside her, purring and rubbing against her skirt.

'You have a better purr than the car engine,' said Mrs Pepperpot. 'Oh, look! There's a pigsty. Let's go and visit the pigs.'

Basking in the sunshine lay a big sow with a whole row of little piglets stretched out beside her. From time to time they woke up, pushed and nudged and sucked and squealed, then they fell asleep again.

Just as she was bending over to stroke the sow, lo and behold! Mrs Pepperpot SHRANK for the second time that day! This was most unusual and quite unexpected.

Luckily, she didn't land among the pigs, but tumbled into a patch of weeds right by the sty.

'Did you hurt yourself? asked a squeaky little voice.

'No, I don't think so, thanks,' said Mrs Pepperpot, struggling to her feet. 'I'm so used to falling—it's almost second nature to me. Hullo! I thought I was talking to a kitten; now I see you're a pig!'

It was indeed a pig, but a very, very small and thin one.

'Don't you belong in there with the others?' asked Mrs Pepperpot.

'I do really. But the farmer put me out. He said my mother had enough to feed and I would have to fend for myself, unless . . .' the piglet put his head on one side and looked wistfully at Mrs Pepperpot from under his white eyelashes, '. . . unless some nice person would take me home and feed me with a bottle.'

'Poor little mite! Does *nobody* want you?'

'Not so far. They all come and look at my mother and the others, gobbling away. But when they see me they just shake their heads and go away,' said the little pig.

'They're stupid and unkind!' said Mrs Pepperpot, 'leaving a fine little fellow like you to starve. I wish I had a bottle of milk handy. If I were my proper size, I'd take you home with me.'

Here the kitten, who had been watching, chipped in: 'You see, Piggy, Mrs Pepperpot isn't always this size—a little while ago she was enormous!'

Mrs Pepperpot laughed. 'I may seem enormous to you, Kitty, but most people call me a *little* old woman. However, what we want right now is to get ourselves over to the farmer's pump. Then, when I grow large again, I can ask if I can have you. My husband's up there too, getting water for his car. But it's too far for me to walk as I am now.'

'I don't think I could carry you,' said the piglet, 'my legs are too wobbly and weak!'

'I'll do what I did before,' said the kitten, 'pull you along by your skirt.'

'Champion!' said Mrs Pepperpot. 'You wait here for us, Piggy. We may be some time, but we'll be back.'

They set off as before, the kitten tugging and pulling Mrs Pepperpot, bumping over the grass and stones. It was hard work up the hill, but the kitten didn't give up till they had reached the pump, where they found the green plastic bucket, but no Mr Pepperpot. He had gone inside to chat with the farmer about the wonders of his old car. They got so interested that when he came out he had forgotten what he came for—to fill his bucket with water.

Mrs Pepperpot, who had hidden inside the bucket when Mr Pepperpot and the farmer came out of the house, wondered if she was going to be left behind. But half-way down the hill Mr Pepperpot remembered the bucket and came rushing back again. The farmer was still standing there: 'You won't get far without water!' he said, as Mr Pepperpot hitched the bucket under the

pump and started pumping.

Poor Mrs Pepperpot! It wasn't very clever of her to hide in the bucket, was it? Now she was in great danger of drowning while Mr Pepperpot went on pumping and talking to the farmer at the same time.

'Travel broadens the mind,' he was saying. 'You need to get out and see for yourself what a beautiful country we live in. D'you know, when I sit behind that wheel with a long clear road in front of me, it often makes me want to sing and shout . . . Ouch!' And he gave a great shout and jumped in the air!

The farmer thought he was showing him what he did when he was driving, but Mr Pepperpot went on jumping about, the bucket fell off the hook and all the water ran out. And Mrs Pepperpot? Well, she had cleverly climbed out of the bucket and had managed to get a hold on Mr Pepperpot's trouser-leg. Then, while he was still talking, she hoisted herself up as far as his braces, but there her foot slipped and she gave him a kick. She also pinched him while trying to stop herself from falling. So that was why Mr Pepperpot shouted: he thought there was an ant inside his shirt.

By now all the rest of the family had come out of the house to look at this funny man dancing round their pump. When he saw they were laughing at him, he ran down the hill to find Mrs Pepperpot and get her to remove the ant, or whatever it was.

But there was no sign of Mrs Pepperpot either in the car or up and down the road.

'Oh dear, oh dear! Now she's shrunk and vanished completely. What shall I do?' After he had hunted around

and called her in vain he suddenly remembered the ant. Heavens! That might have been her! He felt himself all over, but there was no sign of any creepy-crawly now. He would have to go back to the pump. Perhaps he could ask the farmer if he had seen his wife. But how was he going to explain that she might be as small as a tiny doll?

When he got to the pump the whole family was still standing there, so he laughed a little nervously and said: 'I came back for my bucket of water.'

They watched him pump it full again. Then he said: 'Oh, by the way, did you see if I dropped a small doll with a striped skirt on?'

'Doll?' said the farmer. 'No, I didn't see any doll. But I'll ask my wife. Have you seen the gentleman's doll, Kristina?'

'No,' said his wife, 'I didn't see any doll. But I'll ask my daughter. She turned to the eldest girl: 'Have you seen a little doll, Gerda?'

'No,' said Gerda, 'I didn't see any doll. But I'll ask my younger sister, Britta. Did you see a little doll?'

'No,' said Britta, 'but I'll ask my smaller sister, Ada. Did you see a little doll?'

'No,' said Ada, 'but I'll ask my baby sister, Maggie. Did you see a little doll?'

'No,' said Maggie, 'but I'll ask my big brother, Jack. Did you see a little doll?'

'No,' said Jack, 'but I'll ask my bad brother, Ben. Did you see a little doll?'

'No,' said Ben, 'but I'll ask my good brother, Jim. Did you see a little doll?'

'No,' said Jim, 'but I'll ask my sad brother, Frank. Did you see a little doll?'

'No,' said Frank, 'but I'll ask my happy brother, Pete. Did you see a little doll?'

'No,' said Peter, 'but I'll ask my baby brother, John. Did you see a little doll?'

'No,' said Baby John. 'No lil dolly at all!"

'I'm afraid we haven't seen your doll,' said the farmer.

Meanwhile Mr Pepperpot was wringing his hands and muttering to himself: 'I've lost her—this time I really have lost my own dear wife!'

'Did you say *wife*?' asked the farmer with surprise. 'I thought it was a doll you had lost.'

'Well, you see . . . the doll . . . er . . .' Mr Pepperpot didn't know what to say.

'If it's your *wife* you're looking for,' said the farmer, slapping Mr Pepperpot on the back, 'don't worry! We

saw a little old lady in a striped skirt get into your car while you were on your way back here, didn't we, Kristina?'

'Yes,' said his wife, 'and my daughter saw her too, didn't you, Gerda?'

But before the whole family could go through their rigmarole again, Mr Pepperpot was off down the hill, not forgetting the green plastic bucket of water! When he got to the car, there sat Mrs Pepperpot, patiently waiting on the back seat, with her picnic basket on her knee.

Mr Pepperpot was so relieved, he gave her a big kiss. But he couldn't help asking her: 'Did you . . . did you SHRINK?'

'I don't know why you have to keep asking me about

that, Mr P,' said Mrs Pepperpot crossly. 'Try and get that car going for a change!'

This time the car gave no trouble at all, of course. But Mr Pepperpot still felt it would be best to have it checked at the next garage, and Mrs Pepperpot didn't argue, as she wanted to go into the shop right beside it. There she bought a baby's bottle and teat and a pint of milk.

'What do you want that for?' asked her husband when she came back to the car.

'Questions! Questions! When are we going to get to that cross-country race you're so keen to go in for?'

'As a matter of fact, I don't think I *am* so keen now. The man here at the garage has just told me about a fair near here where they have one of those "trials of strength". You know; you hit an iron plate with a big hammer as hard as you can and a disc shoots up to ring a bell. I think I'd like to have a bash at that. You'd like to go to a fair, wouldn't you?'

'I expect so. I might try winning something myself,' said Mrs Pepperpot.

So off they went again: Mr Pepperpot, Mrs Pepperpot, one kitten and one piglet, which, up to now, had kept very quiet.

III

They drove on for a while. Mr Pepperpot kept looking out for posters to show where the fair was being held. In the back seat Mrs Pepperpot had made up a little song to keep them amused. This is how it went:

> 'I know a little pussy-kitten,
> With shiny coat and snowy mitten,
> His ice-cream whiskers wrapped in a rug,
> He's safe inside my basket snug.'

'I like to hear you sing,' said Mr Pepperpot, 'it shows you're feeling happy. I know the tune, too, but I don't remember those words.'

'You're not likely to; I just made them up!' she answered. 'I'll sing you another verse.'

'I know a little piggy pink,
With curly tail and eyes that twink,
His legs are shaky, but no one mocks,
He likes to sit in my old box.'

'It's a funny song, all right, and you're a funny old woman,' said Mr Pepperpot.

'Funny yourself!' said his wife. 'Now I'll sing one about you. Here goes:'

'I know a man who's not a giant,
But very smart and self-reliant.
In motoring he'd spend his life,
He only fears to lose his wife!'

'There!' shouted Mr Pepperpot, slowing down.

'Where? What?' Mrs Pepperpot didn't know what he was talking about.

'There's the fair. Now I can swing the Big Hammer—you'll see; I'll knock that thingummy right to the top—Ping! Let's see,' he got out and read the poster; 'there are lots of other attractions too; sword-swallowers and tight-rope walkers. . . .'

'I'd be careful about swallowing swords, if I were you,' said Mrs Pepperpot, getting out of the car and closing the door to keep her pets in. 'You make enough fuss if you get as much as a herring-bone in your throat!'

'Silly! They're professionals! Well, I'm going this way to the Big Hammer. Why don't you go and look at the circus animals? They say they're as clever as people.' And with that Mr Pepperpot hurried off into the crowd.

The noise was terrific: hurdy-gurdy music from the merry-go-rounds, people screaming on the Big Wheel, Dodgems clanging and the stall-holders all trying to shout each other down.

Mrs Pepperpot felt quite lost, and wondered where she should go. She decided to buy another ice-cream for the kitten and a carton of milk for that hungry piglet. He had been sleeping quietly in his box since she gave him the first bottle, but soon he'd be awake again, and then he might squeal and give the game away.

Just as she reached the kiosk, Mrs Pepperpot felt the ominous signs—'Not again!' was all she had time to say before she shrank and found herself rolling on the ground with huge boots and shoes tramping all around her.

Was she scared! There was danger from every direction, and she was at her wit's end. Should she try to climb up someone's trouser-leg! Before she could make a grab, however, she found herself picked up by her skirt and whisked away from the tramping feet. Whatever it was, it ran so fast that poor Mrs Pepperpot was slung from side to side and completely lost her breath. She tried to shout 'Let me go!', but then she realised it would be better to let herself get carried out of harm's way. Finally, behind a big tent, whatever-it-was stopped and she felt herself lowered carefully on to the grass. Looking up, she saw, standing over her, a furry creature with black, floppy ears and a big moustache.

'Hullo,' she said. 'What are you supposed to be?'

'Oh,' said the creature, 'I'm just me!'

Mrs Pepperpot laughed. 'I see! I ought to have known. Of course, you're a puppy. Perhaps you're one of those clever circus dogs trained to do tricks?'

'No one's going to train me to do tricks!' declared the puppy, shaking his floppy ears vigorously. 'I do what I want and that's that!'

'Quite right,' said Mrs Pepperpot. 'I do what *I* want, too, except when I turn small like I am now. Then I have

to rely on other people's help. If you can help me now, perhaps *I* can help *you* when I grow large. But I can only understand animal language when I am small, so if you've anything to tell me, you'd better do it now.'

Then the puppy told her his story in little excited barks. He really belonged to the circus manager, but when he wouldn't learn to count and to bark in the key of F major, the manager chased him out of his tent.

'But you haven't heard the worst,' added the puppy.

'Let's have it,' said Mrs Pepperpot.

The puppy put his head on one side and looked at her sadly. 'Are you pedigree?' he asked.

'Well,' laughed Mrs Pepperpot, 'I've never really thought about it. I don't think I care if I am or not.'

'As a dog, if you're not pedigree, you're useless, that's what they told me,' said the puppy.

'Never mind! You have a beautiful moustache.'

'They said it didn't belong with my kind of breed.'

'Bother them and their pedigree!' said Mrs Pepperpot. 'That moustache will come in very handy, for you and I are going to fool the whole lot of them!'

The puppy looked at her with big round eyes. 'Why, what are we going to do?'

'You must pick me up very carefully in your mouth, just like you did before,' said Mrs Pepperpot. 'And now jump straight on to the roof of that caravan!'

It was a most tremendous leap, but the puppy arrived safely with Mrs Pepperpot in his mouth. Then Mrs Pepperpot draped his long moustache over her skirts and legs, so that she was completely hidden. At first no

one noticed them up there, but when the music stopped for a pause Mrs Pepperpot suddenly started to sing through the puppy's moustache:

> 'Baa, baa, black sheep,
> Here we go gathering nuts in May,
> Who killed Cock Robin?
> Three blind mice, three blind mice,
> Little Tommy Tucker,
> Sing a song of sixpence,
> Girls and boys come out to play,
> See saw, Marjorie Daw.'

Wasn't that an old jumble of a song? But it was the best she could do, hanging there in mid-air. The people standing round the caravan were astonished to see a puppy on the roof, and even more amazed that he was singing. Others joined them to watch; the roundabout came to a halt, the passengers left the Dodgems, and even the circus performance stopped as the audience flocked outside to hear the clever puppy sing.

The circus manager himself appeared. 'Hi!' he shouted, 'that's my puppy! Here, boy; here, boy!' But the puppy took no notice; it was all he could do to keep his balance with Mrs Pepperpot in his mouth.

'Can you count to ten?' shouted the circus manager. 'One?' No answer. 'Two?' Silence. 'Three? Four? Five?' Still no answer from the puppy. 'You're just having us on, you obstinate little brute! Six, seven, eight, nine, ten . . .'

Mrs Pepperpot decided it was time to teach the circus manager a lesson. In a high, yappy voice she said quickly: 'Eleven, twelve, thirteen, fourteen, fifteen, sixteen, seventeen, eighteen, nineteen, twenty!'

Consternation in the crowd! The circus manager jumped up and down, whooping with excitement. There was such a crush of people trying to see the puppy that they overturned the caravan and everyone fell on top of everyone else! When at last they had sorted themselves out, the puppy had disappeared. He and Mrs Pepperpot had jumped clear when the caravan toppled, and had made for the car as fast as his little legs could carry them.

When Mr Pepperpot returned, his wife, who was now

her proper size, was wrapping something up in an old coat they kept in the back of the car.

Mr Pepperpot was so excited about the singing puppy, he didn't notice what she was doing. 'You should have heard him—he sang a whole song!'

Mrs Pepperpot laughed. 'Get along with you! A dog singing!'

'I saw him with my own eyes!' he assured her. Then he looked thoughtful for a moment and said: 'Come to think of it, it was rather like one of your daft songs!'

'Was it, indeed?' Mrs Pepperpot looked pained. 'How did you get on with the Big Hammer?'

'With all that fuss about the puppy, I didn't get time to try it. Anyway, I heard someone talking about a walking contest. So I thought I'd drive a little further and try that.'

'Very well,' said Mrs Pepperpot with a sigh. She was beginning to wonder if they'd ever get home that day;

if they had to stay overnight somewhere, what would she do with the animals?

But Mr Pepperpot drove happily on, and in the back seat—though he didn't know it—he now had *four* passengers: Mrs Pepperpot, the kitten, the piglet and the puppy with black floppy ears and a big moustache.

IV

When they had driven another few miles Mr Pepperpot stopped the car.

'I don't know what's wrong,' he said, 'but the car seems so heavy at the back. Perhaps the tyres are going flat; I expect I'd better pump them up a bit. You'll have to get out meanwhile.'

Mrs Pepperpot didn't like this idea. If her husband started rummaging in the back of the car he might find the animals.

'I don't feel like getting out just now,' she said. 'Can't it wait till you get to the next petrol station? Then they can do it for you.'

'I suppose so,' he said and drove on. But soon he was grumbling again: 'Why can't you sit still? If there's not

enough room for you in the back seat, you could throw out some of that food.'

He didn't know that the food had been eaten up long ago by the piglet, the kitten and the puppy.

'If anything's to be thrown out, it's not the food!' said Mrs Pepperpot quite huffily. 'If your old car can't even carry one passenger, Mr P, *I* can get out, and you can go on alone!'

This was very cunning of Mrs Pepperpot, because if there is one thing a proud car-owner hates, it is criticism of his beautiful automobile.

'You stay right where you are!' said Mr Pepperpot. 'It's not really the weight that matters, but all the strange noises I have been hearing from the back. I must find out what's causing them.'

'Oh dear!' sighed Mrs Pepperpot, 'that must have been my singing you could hear. I was making up a sort of song—not a proper one, you understand, for *I* have never sung in a choir like *you* . . .'

Mr Pepperpot brightened up at the word 'choir', as he had been very good at choir-singing when he was young.

'That's right, my dear,' he said, 'not everyone is born with a beautiful voice. But you go right ahead and sing; nothing like it for uplifting the soul and making us think of the joys of spring!'

'Don't know so much about the joys of spring,' muttered Mrs Pepperpot, 'it's more like a farmyard when I get going. But you asked for it:

'Dogs are lots of fun,
When they jump and run,
But when they start to yap-yap,
They will get a slap-slap!

Cats are sweet and furry,
Never in a hurry
Till they start a row-row,
Fight and scratch and miaow-miaow!

As for little pigs,
See them dancing jigs;
Their little feet go boink-boink
While their snouts go oink-oink!'

'Ridiculous!' was Mr Pepperpot's comment. 'This time I didn't even know the tune.'

'Nor did I when I started,' said Mrs Pepperpot. 'I can see a petrol station over there.'

'Good,' said Mr Pepperpot. He stopped at the garage and asked the man to pump up his tyres, and Mrs Pepperpot hoped the animals would keep quiet meanwhile. But she needn't have worried, for her husband was soon deep in conversation with the the garage man about a fishing competition which was due to start at two o'clock.

'You can put your name on this list,' the man was

saying, 'and then I'll show you which way to go.'

Mr Pepperpot signed his name to show he was a competitor, and they set off again, this time down a narrow lane through a wood. It was lovely and cool in there and soon they got to a little green glade.

'This is where the man said I could park the car,' said Mr Pepperpot. He got out and fetched his fishing tackle from the boot. 'I suppose you don't want to come and watch me?'

'I'd rather wait for you to bring me back a lovely fish for my supper. I'll just lie in the nice grass and watch the trees for a bit.'

'Bye, bye, then,' said Mr Pepperpot, walking off towards the river, hopeful as ever.

Mrs Pepperpot called 'Good luck!' after him, but as soon as he was out of sight she opened the basket to let the kitten and the piglet out and unrolled the puppy, who had been having a nice nap inside the old coat. They all came tumbling out on the grass. At first the

kitten was a bit frightened and arched his back and hissed at the puppy, but soon they were all three chasing each other round and round. Mrs Pepperpot sat on a tree-stump in the middle and enjoyed the fun. When she thought they had had enough exercise she caught them all and put them back in the car.

'Be good,' she told them. 'I'm going to the shop on the main road to buy some more food for you.' And she shut the car door securely.

It was very pleasant walking along the quiet lane, and

she was quite sorry to get back on to the dusty road. Luckily, the shop wasn't far. It was one of those old-fashioned country stores where they sell everything from pickled herrings in barrels to hair-nets, barbed wire and liquorice. When she got there a lot of people were waiting to be served, so she took a stroll round the back where she found a chicken-yard. She counted twelve

fine hens, pecking and scraping in the sand, but over in a corner stood a miserable little bird, blinking her eyes and shivering. She looked so bedraggled and thin that Mrs Pepperpot at once felt sorry for her.

'You poor thing! But don't you worry; I'll have you out of here in no time, as sure as my name's Pepperpot!'

The little hen didn't seem to hear her, but Mrs Pepperpot went back inside and bought her provisions. When she had finished she asked the little man behind the counter if he would sell her the hen.

'Oh, you don't want that miserable creature!' he exclaimed. 'She's never been any good at laying eggs, and now she's getting old and tough too.'

'We none of us get any younger,' said Mrs Pepperpot, 'and she hasn't had much of a chance, being chased round the yard from morning till night.' As you know, when Mrs Pepperpot makes up her mind she can be very determined, and at last the little man gave in. He found a big cardboard box and put the hen in it. She was so scared she lay absolutely still.

Mrs Pepperpot left the shop with the cardboard box under one arm and the basket of food under the other. It was quite a heavy load for her to carry, and when she reached the lane she put both down, so that she could

change hands and have a rest. Also she wanted to see if the hen was all right. She lifted the lid just a little.

'Mercy!' she shouted, for at that moment she SHRANK for the *fourth* time that day and toppled in with the hen!

More frightened than ever, the bird flapped out of the box, but Mrs Pepperpot managed to cling on to one of her legs. This stopped the hen from flying away.

'Woah!' said Mrs Pepperpot. 'Stand still while I get on your back.' The hen was squawking, and as soon as Mrs Pepperpot was on her back she ran as fast as she could into the bushes, where she got stuck.

'You're a scatter-brain and no mistake!' Mrs Pepperpot told her when they were out in the lane again.

'That's what they've all said—ever since I was born,' said the hen sadly.

Mrs Pepperpot patted her neck. 'I'm sorry, I didn't mean to hurt your feelings. Don't you bother what people say. From now on you're coming to live with me and be my very special feathered friend.'

'Thanks very much, but would you tell me where we are going and how we are going to get anywhere with you such a very small person?'

'Quite right, I should have said. I want you to take me along this lane till we get to my husband's car. I'm not this size all the time, you see, and should be back to normal human size soon.'

'Well, I hope you hurry up, because I can see the fox over there in the bushes!' said the hen, blinking her eyes nervously in that direction. Sure enough! There stood Master Fox, and he was licking his chops.

'Don't worry,' whispered Mrs Pepperpot, 'I'll deal with him!' Out loud she said: 'I see a certain well-known person is out for a walk in the sunshine.'

'That's right. I was giving myself an appetite for my dinner. And I seem to be in luck,' laughed the fox, 'as my dinner is out walking too!' And he made ready to spring on the hen.

'Hold on!' shouted Mrs Pepperpot. 'Don't be in too much of a hurry, Master Fox. You see, I'm going round with invitations to a picnic, so I may as well invite you too. That is, if you'll behave like a gentleman.'

'Very funny!' said the fox, showing his teeth. 'Of course you thought you could trick me like the cockerel once did when he got me to wash my paws before I started eating. I know that one!' He put one paw on the hen, who was trembling all over by now.

But Mrs Pepperpot kept calm. 'I'm not trying to trick you,' she said. 'If you'll let go of the hen at once I promise you'll have a meal much better than a tough old bird. But first I want you to carry the basket of groceries over to that car in the glade. Then you can come back and fetch me and the hen.'

'Oh no!' cackled the hen, more terrified than ever.

'Another trick!' said the fox. 'When I get back you'll both be gone. I want my food *now*!' He put the other paw on Mrs Pepperpot's skirt.

'How stupid you are!' said Mrs Pepperpot. 'I've always heard that foxes were so smart, but that must have been in the old days. If you're afraid of losing us, the hen can carry me on her back and we'll walk beside you all the way.'

The fox agreed. He took the basket in his mouth and the hen carried Mrs Pepperpot on her back till they reached the car. Once there, Mrs Pepperpot asked the fox to unpack the food and sent the hen up on the roof of the car to fetch a plastic tablecloth which they spread on the grass.

'When do we start the feast?' asked the fox.

'We'll have to wait till I collect the rest of the guests,' said Mrs Pepperpot. Then she put her hand to her mouth and shouted with all her might: 'Are you there, Great Cat Tiger-claws?'

'Miaow!' said a little voice from the car.

'What's this?' demanded the fox. 'Are there other guests invited?'

'Oh yes!' answered Mrs Pepperpot, putting her hand to her mouth again. 'Are you there, Wild Boar Gory

Fangs?' she shouted as loudly as she could.

'Oink! Oink!' came the reply from the car.

'Good heavens! Are there any more?' The fox was beginning to look nervous.

'Wait and see!' said Mrs Pepperpot. 'Are you there, Handlebar Moustachio Foxhunter?'

'Woof! Woof!' answered the puppy.

'Thanks very much' said the fox. 'I don't think I fancy this picnic after all!'

'Oh, come on! They'll all be very pleased to see you,' said Mrs Pepperpot. 'You just sit down and enjoy yourself. The hen can sit next to you if you like.'

'I'd rather not!' said the poor hen, who didn't trust the fox one inch.

The fox looked hurt. 'You've tricked me just like the others,' he said. But Mrs Pepperpot shook her head:

'No. I promised you food, and I keep my promises. You can put a large chunk of ham and some fresh eggs in the basket and take it away to eat. Will that satisfy you?'

'Very generous, I'm sure,' said the fox, collecting the food in the basket and picking it up.

Just as he was about to run off with it, Mrs Pepperpot said: 'Just a minute! One thing more. I want the basket back.'

'All right,' said the fox, 'if you can keep your promises,

I can keep mine. I'll see you get it back.' With that he vanished in the bushes, much to the hen's relief.

At that moment Mrs Pepperpot grew to her proper size. She lost no time in getting her pets out and they all had a lovely picnic in the grass. She had just finished putting them back in their different hiding places when Mr Pepperpot returned from his fishing contest. But she could see from his face that there would be no fish for supper *that* night.

'What happened?' she asked.

'Oh,' he said despondently, 'it wasn't much of a turn-out. We had an hour for the contest, but I never got a single bite. And then something very strange happened.'

'What was that?'

'Well, you see this basket?' He held up a basket still wet. 'D'you recognise it?'

'It's our picnic basket,' she said.

'That's right! What I want to know is: how did it come to be floating downstream towards me when you are here, much further down the river?' Mr Pepperpot was scratching his head and looking very puzzled.

Mrs Pepperpot could hardly stop herself from laughing, but she just said: 'I have no idea! How did you get it back?'

'It floated straight on to my line, so I hooked it out.'

'Life's full of surprises, isn't it?' said Mrs Pepperpot, getting back in the car. 'Now let's get on, Mr P, or we'll never get home today.'

So Mr Pepperpot turned the car out of the little glade and drove off with Mrs Pepperpot, the kitten, the piglet, the puppy and the hen all on the back seat.

V

They had not gone many miles when Mr Pepperpot put his foot on the brake and stopped very sharply.

'*Now* what's up?' asked Mrs Pepperpot, who had been having a little doze.

'There's a poster about a contest,' said Mr Pepperpot. 'I want to see what it says.'

'Don't you think we've had enough contests for today? We're getting tired and it's time to go home.'

'Speak for yourself, Mrs P.—I'm not tired,' said Mr Pepperpot.

'Anyway, I wish you wouldn't put the brakes on so suddenly, you should think of us in the back seat,' said Mrs Pepperpot.

'Us? Who's us?' he asked.

'Why . . . er . . . the baggage and me!' Mrs Pepperpot was a little flustered—she had nearly given the game away! But her husband had now got out of the car to look at the poster, and this is what it said:

SENSATIONAL SPORTS EVENT TODAY
The Great Traditional Cross-Country Race
starting from Railway Square at 4 p.m.

The Course is as Follows:
Cross Bilberry Marsh by mapped-out Route,
Wade over Black River above the Waterfall,
Take 12 ft Leap from Red Cliff on the North bank
to White Rock on the South bank. Run to
finishing line at the Big Spruce Tree.
1st Prize a Silver Cup.
Refreshments Served.

'Mercy me!' said Mrs Pepperpot when her husband read it out. 'You're never thinking of entering that one, are you?'

'Well, I don't know,' he said. 'I'd like to watch it anyway.'

'And what are we going to do meanwhile?' she asked.

Mr Pepperpot stared at her. 'You said "we" again!'

'Oh well!' she said crossly, 'you keep stopping and starting, and messing about—is it any wonder if I get mixed up? What am *I* going to do, then? Sit in this stuffy old car?'

'No. As you say you're tired, I'll drop you at the station and you take the train home.'

Mrs Pepperpot thought this over, but then she agreed. 'As long as you leave the car in the station yard and promise me not to take part in the stupid competition,' she said.

He promised and drove the car to the station, where he parked it. He gave Mrs Pepperpot some money to get home and then he went round the other side to the Railway Square to watch the competitors line up for the race.

When he was out of sight Mrs Pepperpot went over to the ticket office. There she bought a ticket for herself and paid for the animals to be put in a wooden crate, so that they could travel in the guard's van. A nice guard helped her get the animals in.

'I'll stay with them till the train comes,' she told the guard, and sat down on the crate. But just as the train pulled up at the platform poor Mrs Pepperpot did her fifth SHRINKING for that day! The crate had wide gaps between the boards, and Mrs Pepperpot fell straight through on to the kitten's tail!

'Miaow!' said the kitten, 'that hurt!'

'Sssh! Don't make a noise,' said Mrs Pepperpot, 'just try and hide me—I don't want the guard to see me like this!'

The animals did their best: the kitten curled his tail over her dress, the puppy spread one ear over her blouse and the hen held one wing carefully over her face. The pig just stretched out beside her and blinked at her from under his white eyelashes. When the guard came back he lifted the crate into the guard's van. Then he looked round for the old woman. Where could she have gone? It was only a little train, so he looked into all the carriages and asked the station-master if he had seen her. She was nowhere.

But the train couldn't wait, so the guard blew his whistle and off they went. The animals were delighted to have Mrs Pepperpot with them. 'How lucky you shrank just now!' they said.

'Well, you'd better make the most of me while you have me,' she told them. 'After five shrinkings in one day I don't suppose it will happen again for a long time. So, if you have any questions, fire away!'

The animals all lined up like a row of school-children with Mrs Pepperpot as their very small teacher standing out in front.

The kitten began: 'Please, ma'am, when do we get to your house?'

'In time for supper,' said Mrs Pepperpot firmly, but to herself she added 'I hope', for she wondered what would happen when they got to their station.

'What am I going to have to eat?' asked the piglet.

'Don't worry, there's a whole bin of lovely mash for piglets at my house,' she assured him.

'What about dogs?' asked the puppy. 'Can I do as I like?"

'Certainly!' said Mrs Pepperpot. 'Liberty Hall, that's what they call my place!'

The hen looked anxiously at her. 'Will there be a lot of other hens in your yard? Will they peck me?'

'You shall be my one and only special hen; didn't I tell you?' said Mrs Pepperpot.

All the animals clapped and flapped and stamped and shouted: 'Hooray for Mrs Pepperpot!'

To keep them from getting too boisterous and to while away the time she decided to teach them a song. 'Listen carefully,' she said, 'and come in when I point to you.' She began to sing.

'Children all, now gather round,
And let us make a jolly sound,
First a dog and then a cat,
A little pig, a hen, all pat!

Here we go: sing as I do,
Puppy dog, a bark from you!
Woof, woof! Woof, woof!'

Here she pointed to the puppy and he barked as loudly as he could: 'Woof, woof! Woof, woof!'

'Here we go: sing as I do,
Little Puss, a song from you!
Miaow, miaow! Miaow, miaow!'

The kitten didn't wait to be asked, but sang in chorus with Mrs Pepperpot: 'Miaow, miaow! Miaow, miaow!'

'Here we go: sing as I do,
Piglet, we must hear from you!
Oink, oink! Oink, oink!'

When Mrs Pepperpot pointed at him, the piglet got so carried away, he wouldn't stop 'oinking', and the puppy had to give him a sharp nip.

'Here we go: sing as I do,
Hennypen, a cluck from you!
Cluck, cluck! Cluck, cluck!'

But the hen was so frightened by all the noise the others had made, she only managed a very small 'cluck, cluck!' the first time. However, they went on practising, and by the time the train stopped at their station they were all singing very well indeed.

The guard opened the door and lifted the crate on to a trolley with a lot of milk-churns. As nobody else got out of the train he blew the whistle and it moved off. Luckily Mrs Pepperpot's name and address were written on the lid, so when Peter, the milkman, came in his van to fetch the churns he saw the crate and thought he was meant to deliver it together with the milk. This saved Mrs Pepperpot a lot of trouble, for as soon as he had put the crate down at the corner of the road leading to her house, and had driven off, there was an almighty CRASH!

Mrs Pepperpot grew so fast that she burst right through the crate, scattering the animals and the boards pell-mell all around. Such a to-do! The hen landed on the branch of a tree, the puppy rolled down the hill, the piglet got his snout stuck in a hole and the poor kitten fell in the stream!

When Mrs Pepperpot had picked herself up she quickly collected all the animals. She put the hen under one arm and the piglet under the other and called the kitten and the puppy to follow her. All together they climbed the hill to her house.

'Here we are, children, home at last!' she said, as she opened the door, and set the hen and the piglet down. The kitten and the puppy trotted in after her and now they were all nosing round to see what their new house was like.

Mrs Pepperpot sat down. She had a problem. Mr Pepperpot was bound to come home soon. How was she going to tell him about the additions to their family? She put her finger on her nose and thought. Then she cried: 'I've got it! I have a solution!'

First she put the kitten in the bed and covered him with the counterpane. Then she put the piglet in the empty wood-box by the stove and sprinkled wood-shavings all over him. The puppy she hid in a basket under the table, and the hen she lifted up on the bureau. 'You keep very still,' she told her, 'I'm going to cover you up.' And she put a large lampshade over her. Then she put the coffee on and went outside to see if her husband was coming.

There he was, struggling up the hill, looking so downcast that she had to shout and wave to him to let him know she was there. When he did see her his whole face lit up and he fairly sprinted up the last bit of the road.

'Am I glad you're here!' he said, giving her a big kiss.

'Why shouldn't I be here, Mr P?' said Mrs Pepperpot. 'What have you done with the car?'

'I couldn't very well take it through the bog and jump it over the river, could I?'

Mrs Pepperpot threw up her hands in horror: 'You never went in for that race, did you? After promising . . .?'

'I know. I only meant to watch it. But then I heard the railway guard asking people if they'd seen a little old woman who was supposed to be travelling on the train to our station. He said she'd disappeared. So, of course, I thought at once it must be you who had turned small.'

'What happened then?' she asked.

'Well, I tried to jump on the train, which was just pulling out, but I couldn't catch it. So I headed straight for Bilberry Marsh. I knew it was a short cut and it would have taken much longer to drive the car round by the road.'

'Go on!' said Mrs Pepperpot, all ears.

'The path across the marsh was clearly marked for the race and it took me straight to the place above the waterfall where you have to wade across. Then I scrambled down the other side till I got to Red Cliff.'

Mrs Pepperpot's eyes were popping out of her head by now: 'You didn't take the twelve-foot leap to White Rock, did you?'

'Of course I did; there was no other way!'

'Then you must have won the race!' said Mrs Pepperpot. 'Did they give you the Prize Cup?'

'I didn't wait for anything like that. All I was thinking about was getting to the station in time to get you out of the train. But I was too late and I thought I'd never see you again.'

'Silly!' said Mrs Pepperpot, but she was wiping her eyes with her apron and sniffing a little. 'Come on in and have some coffee.'

When he was sitting comfortably with his cup of coffee she patted his cheek and said: 'Thanks for the outing. I enjoyed it!'

He smiled. 'I'm glad! And you didn't shrink, did you?'

'Well . . . er . . . actually I did—five times in all.'

'You SHRANK FIVE TIMES???' Mr Pepperpot looked thunderstruck.

Mrs Pepperpot decided to tell him the whole story

'The first time I was very frightened in case you should leave me behind.'

'You know I'd never do that!' said Mr Pepperpot.

She smiled at him. 'No, you wouldn't, would you? Not many people have such kind husbands as *I* have. Well, the first time I shrank I met a kitten. The family he belonged to had gone back to town and left him—just like that—with no food or shelter. Would you have done that?'

'No indeed, that's a terrible thing to do!' said Mr Pepperpot.

'I knew that's how you would feel. So I thought it best to take the kitten along with me. Pussy! Pussy! You can come out now and meet your new master!'

'Miaow!' said the kitten and stuck his little head out from the bedclothes.

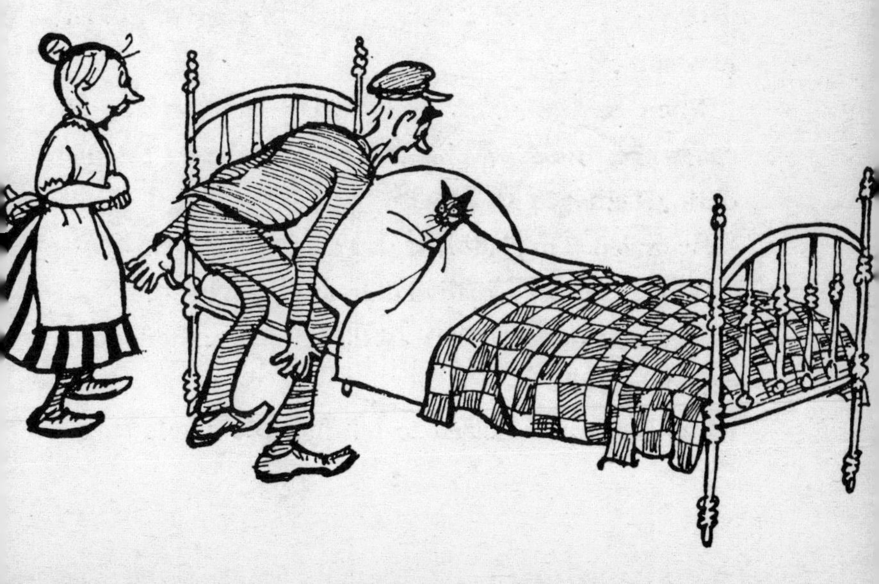

'Well, I'll be . . . !' said Mr Pepperpot. But Mrs Pepperpot was already hurrying him back into the kitchen.

'The second time I shrank,' she said, 'I met a piglet. That was when you went to get water from the pump, remember?'

'So it *was* you and not an ant climbing up my trouser-leg?'

'It was. But never mind that. The little pig had been thrown out by the farmer to fend for himself, and he was so miserable I *had* to help him. I mean, *I've* never had to go hungry in my life—have you?'

'Well, no, I suppose I haven't . . .' said Mr Pepperpot, scratching his head.

'There, you see, I knew you would agree. Come on, Piggy, show yourself to Mr Pepperpot!' And out of

the shavings in the wood-box came first a pair of pink ears, then a little pink snout and lastly a whole pink piglet.

'Good gracious!' said Mr Pepperpot.

'But that's not all,' said his wife. 'The third time I shrank was at the fair. There I was, right on the ground under all those people's feet . . .'

Mr Pepperpot was holding his ears. 'Stop! Don't tell me! One of these days you'll get yourself killed.'

'Ah, but I was rescued by a very clever puppy, one that had you all gasping with his singing and his counting.'

'*No!* You don't mean to say that that was you as well?'

Mrs Pepperpot nodded. 'But I think it's more important that a dog should be a real dog and not learn circus tricks —a dog that can be your friend and protect you.'

'You mean we ought to have a guard dog?' said Mr Pepperpot.

'That's right, and I have the very one. Out you come, Puppy! Show your master how clever you are!'

'Woof! Woof!' barked the puppy excitedly, as he danced round Mr Pepperpot's feet.

'You see, he's your friend already," said Mrs Pepperpot, as her husband bent down to pat the floppy black ears and pull that long moustache.

'Good dog!' he said.

'The fourth time was when you were fishing. I had gone to the shop for some groceries, and I bought a hen because she didn't lay eggs.'

'Because she *didn't* lay eggs?' Mr Pepperpot was getting quite confused.

'Well no, you see, she was being hen-pecked by all the other birds in the yard, so she didn't really have a chance.'

'Cluck-cluck-cluck-alooooh!' The sound came from under the lampshade. Mrs Pepperpot hurried to take it off, and there stood the hen on the bureau, and under her lay a large, brown egg!

Mr Pepperpot burst out laughing: 'She's certainly making up for lost time!'

'She laid it specially for you!' said Mrs Pepperpot, 'because you're the kindest and most understanding of husbands, and all the animals love you!'

'Steady on!' protested Mr Pepperpot. 'You know very well it's you the animals love. You must have the first egg!'

'I don't care what you say, this one's going to be fried for you!' And she cracked it on the edge of the frying-pan while Mr Pepperpot watched. Into the hot fat fell two golden yolks!

'That hen knows how to keep the peace,' said Mr Pepperpot, 'now we can each have an egg!'

When they had had their supper Mrs Pepperpot said: 'I have one more surprise for you.'

Mr Pepperpot groaned: 'Not another animal, I hope.'

'Come into the parlour and I'll show you,' she said and opened the door. There on the table stood a brightly polished silver cup.

'That's for you!' she said. 'You've certainly earned it today.'

'But that's the cup you won for handling livestock when you were a young girl working on the farm!'

'Well, I give it to you now because you're just as good at handling livestock!' answered Mrs Pepperpot.

'I suppose we could hold it jointly . . .?' suggested Mr Pepperpot.

'That's a very good idea. And now, have you thought what you will do with the rest of your holiday?' she asked him.

'I can't say I have, but I don't think I'll do any more motoring.'

'Good!' said Mrs Pepperpot, 'I think it's very nice to stay at home sometimes. And then you can get out your tool-box and build a pen for the piglet, a run for the hen, a kennel for the dog and . . .'

'And *nothing* for the cat!' said Mr Pepperpot firmly. But the kitten didn't mind; he was already stretched out in his favourite spot—along the top of Mr Pepperpot's armchair.

Mrs Pepperpot has a Visitor from America

IT'S not so often that there's a letter in the post for Mrs Pepperpot. But one day when she opened her letter-box she found a big letter with many foreign stamps on it. It was from her sister who lives in St. Paul, Minnesota, U.S.A., and this is what it said:

Dear Sister,

I am now on my way to the Old Country and would like to visit you. Can you come and meet me at Fornebu Airport? That will make me very, very happy.

Your loving sister, Margret Anne

'Well, well!' said Mrs Pepperpot to herself, 'so my loving sister is coming back to Norway? It must be forty years since we last saw each other and there wasn't much loving sister about her then. As I remember it, I always got the short end of the stick. We'd go to the store and it would be little me to carry the basket while Miss Hoity Toity Margret Anne talked with the boys. And at school . . . I shall never forget the day she said I'd spilt ink over her copy-book and ruined it. As if I'd do a thing like that! Then there was the other time she fell in the brook and said I'd pushed her in. If we went blueberry picking she'd pinch my basket because it was full and she was too lazy to get her own. And then . . .'

But we won't go on listening to all this miserable stuff, because it's quite clear that Mrs Pepperpot was in a very bad mood that day. All the same, her sister would have to be met at the airport; there was no getting away from that!

'I'll go,' said Mrs Pepperpot, 'but if Margret Anne thinks I'm going to doll myself up for her sake, she's much mistaken! I'll put on some old clothes of our mother's and a shawl round my head, and I'll take my broom along. Then my fine sister may not even want to know me!'

The day came and Mrs Pepperpot took the bus to the airport. It was quite a long trip and the other passengers were a bit surprised to see her get on in her old-fashioned clothes and carrying a broom.

At the airport there was a great crowd of people, and they stared even more at the little old woman with her shawl and her broom. Some of them were talking in foreign languages, and everyone was carrying heavy suitcases and pushing this way and that. By the time the loudspeaker announced that the plane from New York was about to land, Mrs Pepperpot was so confused, she didn't know if she was standing on her head or her heels. As it happened, it didn't matter very much, because at that moment she SHRANK!

'Oh my goodness!' wailed Mrs Pepperpot, as she rolled along the slippery floor and very nearly got trodden on,

'What a time for this to happen!'

But almost at once she felt herself snatched up by a large lady's hand and popped into a glass show-case.

'Somebody must have been trying to steal one of the souvenirs,' said the large lady and locked the door of the show-case.

There stood Mrs Pepperpot, shawl, broom and all! She could see the people coming in from the plane, and among them, looking anxiously round, was a lady in a smart fawn hat and flowers on her coat and dress which matched the flowers on her outsize handbag. She wore spectacles with jewelled rims which sparkled most amazingly.

'That must be Margret Anne,' thought Mrs Pepperpot, and a moment later she was sure, because the lady walked past the show-case talking aloud to herself:

'Oh dear, where can my sister be? I'd better wait a bit.'

She came back and looked into the show-case.

'Maybe I should buy some Norwegian souvenirs for my friends in America. Oh, what a wonderful doll! She looks just like my mother with that shawl, and she used to have a broom just like that. But the face isn't like her—oh no, it has such a bad-tempered expression!'

Mrs Pepperpot was fuming inside: 'Has it indeed! I wonder what your mother would say if she could see *you*, dressed up as you are, in your American finery!'

Margret Anne went on talking to herself: 'I really must buy that doll to show my sister; she'll think it very, very funny!'

Mrs Pepperpot didn't think it funny at all, but held herself as stiff as she could while the large lady picked her up and gave her to Margret Anne, who paid for her and put her in her outsize handbag. Before it was closed, Mrs Pepperpot had time to see what a lot of knick-knacks there were inside: powder compact, lipsticks, paper hankies, face-cream, notebooks, pens and pencils, cigarettes. . . . Once the lid was closed Mrs Pepperpot was almost suffocated with all the different smells and she badly wanted to sneeze. But she kept as still as a mouse while her sister called a taxi.

Margret Anne told the taxi-man to drive all the way to the valley where Mrs Pepperpot lived, which was many miles away.

'That'll cost her a pretty penny!' thought Mrs Pepperpot. 'But at least I'll get a free ride.'

The taxi drove on and on, and Mrs Pepperpot must have had a little snooze, because suddenly she woke up to hear her sister say: 'Driver! Stop at this shop, please! I haven't been here since I was a child, and I want to go in and buy a few things for my sister. When she was a little girl she was always so good about carrying the groceries home for me.'

'Well, I never!' said Mrs Pepperpot inside the handbag.

Margret Anne went up to the counter and bought some smoked fish, some goat-milk cheese and some strong Norwegian sausage.

'I haven't tasted these things for forty years,' she told the grocer, who was a young man and didn't remember Margret Anne. She put all the things in her handbag on top of poor Mrs Pepperpot.

'Pooh!' said Mrs Pepperpot. 'I'll die if I have to stay in this smelly bag much longer!'

Just as she was going out of the shop, Margret Anne asked the grocer if he had a small bottle of ink.

'Good gracious! What does she want that for?' thought Mrs Pepperpot, as the ink bottle was poked into a corner beside her.

Then she heard her sister ask the taxi-man to drive to the school-house.

'I want to look at the room where my sister and I learned our lessons. It's all so long ago, but I've often thought how unkind I was when I told the teacher my sister poured ink on my copy-book.'

'I see!' thought Mrs Pepperpot. 'The bottle of ink is a peace-offering. Better late than never!'

When she had looked inside the little old school-room, Margret Anne asked the driver to stop a short way out of the village where there was a bridge over the brook.

'You see, that's where I once fell in when I was a child and I told my mother that my sister pushed me.'

'I got a good hiding for that, my fine lady!' said Mrs Pepperpot inside the bag.

'I'd like to sit on the bridge for a moment and think about how wicked I was. D'you think my sister will have forgiven me?'

The taxi-man laughed: 'Why, ma'am,' he said, 'she'll

be so pleased to see you after all these years, she won't worry about your little tiffs when you were young!'

'Perhaps she's not so bad, after all,' thought Mrs Pepperpot.

Margret Anne was dangling her legs over the edge of the bridge and staring down into the water, when suddenly she saw a great fish swimming by. She got so excited, she dropped the handbag into the brook!

'Help, help!' cried Mrs Pepperpot, as the bag went whirling downstream. She was rolling round and round inside with the cheese and the fish and, worst of all, the ink! The cap had come off and she was covered in the

stuff. Luckily the bag hit a stone which forced the catch open and Mrs Pepperpot was thrown out.

Remembering a diving lesson a frog had given her once, she went in head first to clean off the ink, and then she swam to the bank, pulling the bag after her.

'Now if only I could get back to my proper size!' she said, and, for once, it actually happened as she wished.

She was not far from home, so she ran up the hill as fast as she could go and into her house.

When Margret Anne arrived a few minutes later in the taxi, there stood her sister to greet her at the door, wearing a nice clean frock and with her hair neatly combed.

'Aw, honey! It's good to see my little sister after all

these years!' cried Margret Anne, as she flung her arms round Mrs Pepperpot's neck.

'Little is right,' thought Mrs Pepperpot, but all she said was: 'You're very welcome, Margret Anne, I'm sure.' She could see the taxi-man was grinning as he turned the car down the hill.

'Come on in and make yourself at home!' she went on, and led her sister indoors where the table was laid with strawberry layer-cake and pancakes with blueberry jam.

Margret Anne walked round admiring everything and saying how wonderful it was to be home. Then she remembered the lost handbag.

'It just fell out of my hand,' she told Mrs Pepperpot, 'and the water was running so fast it disappeared before we could catch it, though the driver did his best. I had everything in it, except my money, but what I'm really sorry about, honey, was a little old doll, dressed in a long black skirt with a shawl over its head and carrying a broom. It looked so like our mother—you'd have died laughing!'

'Is this the handbag!' asked Mrs Pepperpot, shyly holding up a large wet object that was still dripping on the floor. 'I got out of it—I mean, I *found* it—just down below the hill. But the doll has gone, I'm afraid.'

'How sad!' said Margret Anne, 'and the bag is a wreck!'

To console her sister, Mrs Pepperpot brought out one of those plastic dolls, dressed in the latest American fashion and with a pair of jewelled spectacles on just like Margret Anne. How they both laughed! And as they were hungry after all their adventures, they sat down to eat the delicious pancakes and layer-cake.

'I haven't tasted anything so good for forty years,' declared Margret Anne. Then she looked at Mrs Pepperpot and said: 'It's funny, sister, but I always thought of you as such a small person.'

Mrs Pepperpot grinned: 'There are times when I feel pretty small myself!'

Gapy Gob gets a Letter from the King

IT'S time we had a story about ogres. D'you remember we met some before?

There was a he-ogre who was called Gapy Gob, because he was so fond of eating he always had his mouth open for more. Then there was a she-ogre, or ogress, whose name was Wily Winnie, because she was always up to some trick or other.

Gapy Gob had two of the nicest little servants: a girl who did the cooking and was called Katie Cook and a boy who chopped the wood, so he was called Charlie Chop. *They* weren't ogres at all, just ordinary children, but they had no home of their own, so they lived with Gapy Gob, and he was very, very fond of them. Wily Winnie also had a servant, a very cunning cat called Ribby Ratsoup.

Gapy Gob and the children lived on the sunny side of a small mountain in a cosy little house with a cow-shed. They had one brown cow, but she only spent the winter in the shed, all spring and summer she grazed on the

high mountain pasture and gave them wonderful milk. While Charlie Chop kept the yard stocked with dry logs to burn on the stove, Katie Cook looked after the garden and saw that they always had plenty of potatoes and other vegetables. If it hadn't been for one thing, they would all three have been as happy and contented as kings.

But on the dark side of the mountain, where the sun never shone, lived Wily Winnie in her dark, untidy mess of a house. Her cat, Ribby Ratsoup, was so lazy that she never swept the floor or made their beds, but if she saw her chance to steal a nice bit of meat or fish, she made a huge steaming bowl of stew (don't ask me what *else* she put in it) and they lived on it for days.

Now these two envied Gapy Gob his nice house and especially his well-stocked larder. For Katie was such a good cook and housewife that she always had a large ham hanging up in the larder and a great bowl of milk with thick cream on top standing on the shelf.

Wily Winnie would have given the last remaining tooth in her big ugly mouth to have a taste of that lovely ham, and Ribby Ratsoup's whiskers trembled when she thought of dipping into that layer of golden cream! But it was no use, Katie always locked the door of the larder very carefully and hung the key on a belt round her waist.

So the ogress and her cat sat in their dark little kitchen and schemed and schemed till one morning in May Ribby came up with an idea.

A little while later, when Charlie Chop was standing in Gapy's yard, chopping wood as usual, he heard a rustling in the wheatfield close by.

'Who's treading down our young wheat?' he asked

loudly. He was pretty sure he knew who it was.

Right enough, out of the corn stalked Ribby Ratsoup with her tail in the air.

'It's only little me,' she minced, and tried to slip past Charlie. But he blocked the cat's way with the axe and demanded sternly: 'What d'you want, you good-for-nothing sly-puss?'

'Tut, tut! Such language!' said Ribby, getting up on her hind legs and dusting herself down. 'I have business with your master which doesn't concern you. Is he at home?'

'Maybe he is and maybe he isn't,' said Charlie, 'but he has no business with *you*, so you can just skip off home!'

'What a very rude servant Gapy Gob keeps,' said Ribby with her nose in the air. 'I shall have to tell him about you. Anyway, I have a letter for him from the King.'

'Rubbish,' said Charlie. 'The King wouldn't send a scruffy cat like you with a letter to my master.'

'That's enough!' said Ribby. 'Actually the postman asked me to deliver the letter, as I was coming this way, and now will you please let me pass!'

So Charlie allowed the cat to go inside the house, where she found Katie at the stove, busy stirring a pot of porridge for Gapy Gob's breakfast.

'Good morning and good appetite!' said Ribby, trying to curtsey with her stiff back legs.

'Good appetite is right,' said Gapy Gob, who was sitting at the table, drumming with his wooden spoon. He was very hungry and didn't like to be kept waiting for his meals.

Katie said nothing, but Ribby walked round the table, purring in her cattiest way: 'Don't worry, Gapy Gob,' she said, 'you'll soon have the most scrumptious porridge. We all know what a good cook Katie is. Of course, in our house we do have breakfast rather earlier, my mistress is so very particular!'

'In this house we eat when the food is ready,' said

Katie crossly, 'and it's no later today than it usually is. Anyhow, what d'you want, Ribby? There are no herrings for you to run off with today, if that's what you're after!'

'What an idea!' said Ribby. 'You and Charlie must both have jumped out of bed the wrong side this morning!' Then she turned her back on Katie and gave Gapy Gob one of those smiles that reach from ear to ear.

'I've brought something for you,' she said.

'What is it?' asked Gapy Gob, who loved getting presents.

'The postman asked me to deliver this letter to you personally,' said Ribby, as she pulled a big envelope from her apron pocket. 'It's from the King.'

Gapy Gob's eyes grew as round as saucers. 'From the King?' he stammered. 'What does he want with me?'

'Let me see,' said Katie, trying to snatch the letter from Ribby.

But Ribby showed her claws and hissed: 'Keep your fingers to yourself, Miss Hoity Toity. The King's writing is so fine it can only be read by cat's eyes.'

'Read it to me, Ribby, there's a good cat,' said Gapy coaxingly, 'and you, Katie, just get on with the porridge.'

Ribby Ratsoup opened the envelope and pulled out a sheet of paper.' "To Mr Gapy Gob from His Majesty the King," ' she began importantly.

' "As it has come to our notice that Mr Gapy Gob has

been eating more ham and cream—as well as more porridge—than is good for him, we hereby decree that he must from now on live on butter toffees exclusively. . . ." '

'Exclu—whatever-it-is, what does that mean?' asked Gapy Gob.

'To anyone who has had schooling like myself,' said Ribby, twirling her whiskers and looking slyly at poor Katie at the stove, 'it is quite simple. It means that you can only eat butter toffees and *nothing* else at all!'

'Mm, I wouldn't mind that!' said Gapy Gob, who was already licking his chops.

'Can I go on?' asked Ribby.

'Oh yes, please do,' said Gapy.

' "Whatever ham and cream is now in Mr Gapy Gob's larder must be handed over to Madam Wily Winnie immediately. Signed H.M. King." '

Quick as a flash Katie took the letter from Ribby's hand. The writing was so small she couldn't read it and as for the signature, it looked more like a cat's cradle!

'It's all nonsense!' she told Gapy. But he wouldn't listen; he was sure the letter came from the King, and, besides, he liked the idea of eating butter toffees for a change.

'Did the King send any toffees for me?' he asked.

'No,' said Ribby, 'but, as it happens, I have some in my

apron pocket. Here you are!' And she poured a whole pile of toffees in coloured paper wrappings on to the table. 'I'll have to go home to my mistress now, but we'll be back this afternoon for the ham and the cream!'

'Mind you bring some more toffees!' said Gapy Gob, who was already munching three, 'I won't get far with this little handful!'

Ribby promised to bring lots more toffees, and bounded off into the wheatfield, ploughing a great path through the corn, while Charlie Chop tried to hit her with a log of wood.

Inside the house Katie was standing in front of Gapy Gob, her hands on her hips: she was very angry. 'Fancy you believing all that stuff!' she said.

But Gapy Gob was munching his eighth toffee and finding it very, very good. 'The King knows what's best for me,' he said, with his mouth full, 'and nothing you can say will make any difference. You can throw all that porridge out of the window—or eat it yourself, if you like. Just give me my plate and I'll eat the rest of the toffees with a spoon.'

Just then Charlie came in for his breakfast.

'What's Gapy Gob eating?' he asked his sister.

'Butter toffees that Ribby gave him,' she said, 'and he's not even bothering to take off the paper.'

'But you know toffee is bad for his teeth!' said Charlie. 'Anyway, what's wrong with porridge?'

'The King has forbidden me to eat porridge—or ham—or cream; I'm just to eat toffees and it's wonderful!' said Gapy Gob, grinning at them both between munches.

Well, the children gave up after that. They just ladled out some porridge into their own little wooden bowls and ate it up without another word.

By now Gapy Gob had eaten twenty-eight butter toffees and was just starting on his twenty-ninth when suddenly he threw down his spoon and gave a loud wail. 'Ouch!' he shouted, 'it hurts!'

Katie and Charlie took no notice, but just went on eating.

'Ouch!' he shouted again, holding his face in his

hands: 'Can't you see I'm in pain, children? Do something about it!'

'What can *we* do?' asked Katie. 'You'd better write a letter to the King.'

'Or send for Wily Winnie and that clever cat of hers!' said Charlie.

'Don't be like that!' said Gapy Gob, and he put his head on his arms on the table and started to cry. 'I tell you it hurts like anything!' he sobbed.

'Oh, very well,' said Katie to Charlie, 'I suppose we'll have to help him. You bring that scrubbing brush and we'll take him down to the waterfall.'

'What are you going to do with me?' asked poor Gapy Gob.

'Come along now, and don't ask questions,' said Katie, helping him to his feet and leading him outside. Then they took him down to a place where there was a little waterfall over some rocks.

'Now,' said Katie, 'you sit down and lean your head back under the waterfall. That's right!' she said, as Gapy Gob obediently held his head under the rushing water.

'Now open your mouth!' said Katie, and she beckoned to Charlie to start brushing Gapy's teeth. The scrubbing brush was just right, as Gapy's mouth was almost the size of a hippopotamus's.

Poor Gapy Gob! He was nearly choking with the water

pouring into his mouth, and the scrubbing brush tasted of soap and disinfectant, but very soon it was over, and all the sweet, sticky toffee had been washed away.

Katie had brought a towel to dry him with. While he was sitting on the rock she could reach his head, and she rubbed and rubbed till he was quite dry. But Gapy Gob was still unhappy. 'It hasn't stopped hurting! Look, in there, that tooth!' and he pointed inside his mouth.

Charlie climbed on the ogre's knee and peeped in; sure enough, one tooth had a big hole in it!

'No wonder it hurts!' he said. 'I'll soon fix that!' And he went over to a tree-stump and pulled off a big lump of resin (that's the gummy stuff that oozes out of trees). He rolled in into a nice ball in his fingers—just like the dentist does—and plugged it into Gapy's tooth.

'That's better,' said Gapy Gob, 'it's stopped hurting altogether!' Then they all went back to the house and the ogre thanked both his faithful servants.

'I never want to see another butter toffee in all my life,' he declared, 'and I don't care *what* the King says!'

'It's not the King you have to worry about,' said Katie. 'What about Wily Winnie and Ribby Ratsoup who are coming here this afternoon to fetch the ham and the bowl of cream?'

'Oh dear, oh dear, I'd forgotten about that!' wailed Gapy Gob. 'What shall I do?'

'Don't worry,' said Charlie, 'we'll find a way to fix those two minxes.'

So, in the afternoon, when the ogress and her servant, the cat, arrived, they were ready for them.

Wily Winnie and Ribby Ratsoup were a bit nervous. 'You knock!' said Wily to the cat.

'No, you do it!' said Ribby, and then the door opened

and they both fell into the kitchen in a heap.

'Hullo!' said Gapy Gob, and gave them both a pleasant smile.

Wily Winnie picked herself up. 'We've just come for . . .' and then she didn't know what more to say.

But Katie helped her out. 'Oh yes,' she said, 'we've packed up the ham in a paper parcel and put a cloth over the cream bowl, so that it won't upset when you carry it. Here it is, all ready for you on the table. We hope you will enjoy it as much as our master enjoyed the toffees. Did you bring him some more toffees?'

'Oh, no!' cried Gapy Gob. backing into a corner. 'No more toffees—ever!'

'Well . . . Thank you very much!' said the ogress. 'We'll be off home then. Come on, Ribby, you carry the cream.' And she took the large paper parcel from the table and walked out, followed by Ribby, carefully balancing the covered bowl between her paws.

As soon as they were out of sight of the house, Wily turned to Ribby. 'Let me have a taste of your cream,' she said, and put out her hand for the bowl.

'Oh no,' said Ribby, holding on to the bowl, 'not till you give me a slice of your ham!'

In the tussle that followed, the bowl fell on the ground and the contents started running down the road.

'Look what you've done!' shouted Ribby.

'How dare you answer me back!' shouted Wily Winnie, and she hit the cat over the head with the paper parcel. It gave a great crack, and out flew—not a ham, but an old broom with a broken handle!

'Of all the dirty tricks!' said the ogress, and stamped her foot so hard it made the ground tremble.

But Ribby was down on all fours, trying to save some of the cream by licking it up. She took one taste and then she spat it out, right into Wily Winnie's face!

'It's white paint!' she hissed. 'We've been double-crossed!'

Much later, when Gapy Gob and the children went for their evening walk to watch the sun go down, they could see Wily Winnie many miles away, running up and down the mountain, still chasing her cat with that old broom! And they laughed and they laughed and they laughed!

Mrs Pepperpot and the Budgerigar

NEAR Mrs Pepperpot's house stands a very pretty little cottage with a garden round it. There is also a handsome double gate decorated with trees and flowers and leaves, all made of wrought iron and painted shiny black. Entwined in the leaves on one side of the gate is the word 'Happy' and on the other the word 'Home'. So when the gate is shut it reads 'Happy Home'. As a matter of fact, the cottage belongs to a Mr and Mrs Happy. The wife's first name is Bella, but no one's ever heard the husband's first name, as he hardly ever speaks to anyone, but just sits under the sunshade in the garden and reads his newspaper. Mrs Pepperpot thinks 'Mr Glum' would have suited him better.

The Happys are only there in the summer holidays, but then Mrs Pepperpot sees quite a lot of Mrs Happy. She pops over to borrow a bit of rhubarb or a cup of flour, or to snip a few chives or some parsley. This goes on nearly every day, and they always have a little chat and then Mrs Happy says: 'You really must come and visit

me one of these days and meet my Pipkins—he is such a darling bird!'

Pipkins is Mrs Happy's budgerigar, which she brings with her from town, so that he too can have a nice country holiday.

'He's getting so clever at talking,' said Mrs Happy one day. 'I've taught him to say four whole words now. As soon as I have a free day, Mrs Pepperpot, I'll invite you over.'

Mrs Pepperpot had never seen a budgerigar and was very curious to hear a bird talking, so she thanked Mrs Happy and hoped she'd soon be asked.

But the days went by, and although Mrs Happy still kept coming over for this and that which she'd forgotten to buy at the store, she always seemed to be too busy to invite Mrs Pepperpot to her house.

Then one morning Mrs Pepperpot had been picking sugar-peas for her husband's supper and she found she had quite a lot over.

'I could take them over to Mrs Happy,' she said to herself. 'Then perhaps she would let me have a look at that budgery—thing-e-me-jig. I'd dearly like to hear a bird talk.'

So she put on her best apron and scarf, popped the peas in a paper bag and walked over to 'Happy Home'. She went through the wrought-iron gate, up the path and through the open front door. Inside the hall she knocked on one of the closed doors. No one answered, but she

could hear Mrs Happy talking to someone inside.

'Come on, darling,' she was saying, 'just to please me, say "Thank you, Mama!" '

'That's funny,' thought Mrs Pepperpot, 'I never knew Mrs Happy had any children.' She knocked again.

'Wait a minute, my love,' said Mrs Happy inside, 'there's someone at the door.' And she opened the door just a tiny crack.

'Oh, it's you, Mrs Pepperpot,' she said, slipping through the door and shutting it behind her. 'How kind of you to call.'

'I just brought you these peas from the garden,' said Mrs Pepperpot and handed her the bag.

'Thank you so much; I love sugar-peas!' said Mrs Happy. 'I wish I could ask you in, but just now I'm busy with my little boy . . .'

'You never told me you had a son,' said Mrs Pepperpot.

Mrs Happy laughed. 'Oh dear, no, I mean my Pipkins, my little budgie! He's all I have, you know, and just now I'm making him practise the words he can say, so that my friends can hear him when they come to tea this afternoon. They're coming all the way from town.'

'Well, I'll be going then,' said Mrs Pepperpot, who was a bit disappointed at not being asked in.

'Come round tomorrow morning,' said Mrs Happy, 'and have a cup of coffee and help me finish up the cakes.'

When she got home Mrs Pepperpot remembered that she hadn't time next morning, as that was her washing day.

'I'll slip over later and tell her I can't come,' she said to herself. So, about three o'clock, she walked over to the cottage and again she found the front door open, so she went into the hall and knocked on one of the inner doors. As there was no reply, she opened the door and found herself in the sitting-room. It was all ready for the tea-party, she could see, with a pretty white cloth on the table, the best china set out and a big vase of flowers. On a smaller table by the window stood a cage.

Mrs Pepperpot couldn't resist going over to have a look at the pretty blue bird which was swinging to and fro on its perch. She sat down on the table beside the cage and said: 'Hullo, Pipkins, are you going to talk to me?'

The bird just looked at her.

'I don't believe it *can* talk!' said Mrs Pepperpot, and as she said that she felt herself SHRINK!

'So you don't believe I can talk,' said the budgerigar, but now, of course, he was talking bird-language, which Mrs Pepperpot could understand when she grew small.

'Well,' said Mrs Pepperpot, 'I hadn't *heard* you talking till now.' She was standing on the table, wondering how she was going to get away before Mrs Happy and her guests came in.

'As a matter of fact,' said the bird, 'you've come just at the right moment. I want you to help me.'

'Help *you*? How can I help you when I don't even know how to help myself just now?' said Mrs Pepperpot, walking all round the cage to see if there was anything she could climb down by. But she was trapped!

'Well, I want to play a trick on Mrs Happy,' said the bird.

'A trick, Pipkins, what sort of a trick?' asked Mrs Pepperpot.

'Please don't call me by that stupid name. Pipkins, indeed; my real name is "Suchislife". Don't you think that sounds more superior?' The budgerigar was preening his feathers as he spoke, and looking down his beak at Mrs Pepperpot.

'Oh yes,' she said hurriedly, 'very superior!' Secretly she thought it sounded like something her husband usually said when he hadn't won the ski-race: 'Ah well, such is life!'

'What d'you want me to do?' she asked the bird.

'I'll explain,' said Suchislife. 'But we must be quick, as Mrs Happy has only gone down the hill to meet her guests. First, will you open the door of the cage, please?'

Mrs Pepperpot did as she was asked and unhinged the cage door.

'Now, just step inside,' went on the bird, and Mrs Pepperpot walked into the cage.

No sooner was she in than the budgerigar hopped out and, quick as lightning, fastened the door-hinge with his beak!

'Got you!' he chirped merrily and flapped his wings with excitement.

Mrs Pepperpot glared at him through the bars. 'You needn't think you can be funny with me!' she said, 'or I shall take back my offer to help!'

'Sorry, ma'am!' he said. 'When I get my freedom it sort of goes to my head, don't you know. But please don't be angry; just listen to my plan.' He had flown up on top of the cage, and took hold of the cover which was hooked on to it. 'I'm going to put the cover on,' he said, as he pulled it neatly down over the cage with his beak, making it quite dark for Mrs Pepperpot inside.

'Now,' said the bird, 'Mrs Happy won't notice that you're in there instead of me. She'll want me to do my party piece to impress her precious guests, so when you hear her say: "Come on, pet, say 'Thank you, Mama' and 'Pipkins Happy'," you just tell her what you think of her.'

'But you haven't told me why you don't like her,' objected Mrs Pepperpot.

'She's mean, and for all her talk about how clever I am, she neglects me. I often have to go without fresh water or she forgets to give me any grain. But you'll soon see what she's like.' And with that Suchislife flew out of the window and hid in a tree to watch what would happen.

Mrs Pepperpot had just settled herself comfortably on the budgerigar's swing when she heard the ladies come into the sitting-room.

'D'you think it can really talk?' she heard one of them say.

'Four words; think of that!' said the second lady.

'Wonderful, isn't it?' said the third lady.

Mrs Pepperpot didn't know what to do. She could hear Mrs Happy getting the tea ready in the kitchen, and now she heard the ladies coming nearer the cage.

'Shall we have a peep at it?' asked the first lady.

'D'you think we dare?' said the second.

'We could just lift the cover a little bit,' suggested the third.

But at the moment a little voice from inside the cage squeaked: 'Don't touch the cover!'

'How very strange,' said the first lady. 'It said four words exactly. Mrs Happy! Your budgie has just talked to us—we heard it clearly.'

Mrs Happy came in with the cakes; she was so taken up with getting the tea served, that she didn't ask *what* words the bird had said. She didn't even notice the cover was on.

'My Pipkins is so clever! Now do sit down all of you and make yourselves at home.' And they all sat down and started chattering the way ladies do, and Mrs Pepperpot stayed as quiet as if she had really been a budgerigar under the cover. But she listened to every word that was being said.

'I must tell you,' said Mrs Happy, laughing gaily, 'about the funny neighbour I have just down the road. She's a little old woman with long skirts and a shawl, and she wears her hair scraped back like something from Grandma's time. She's a scream! She will come tripping in here, knocking at the door . . .'

From the cage came an indignant squeak: 'You invited her yourself!'

For a moment Mrs Happy didn't know what to say, but then she laughed again: 'Isn't he funny? You'd almost think he was joining in the conversation, but, of course, he doesn't know what he's saying. I'll get him to say his name, but first I'll take the cover off so you can see him.' And she got up to do this.

'Don't touch the cover!' squeaked the voice from the cage.

'That's what it said before!' said one of the ladies.

'How very odd!' said Mrs Happy. 'Perhaps someone else has been teaching him to talk while I was out. Well, we won't bother with him just now. I was telling you about the funny old woman down the road; she has the quaintest little house . . .'

'That's not what you say when you go borrowing rhubarb and sugar and eggs and parsley and anything else you've forgotten to buy. The little old woman's good enough for that, Mrs Snobby Happy!'

All the ladies were aghast. Mrs Happy jumped up and ran to the table to snatch off the cover. But her foot slipped and she fell, knocking the whole cage out of the open window!

While the ladies screamed and picked up Mrs Happy, Suchislife flew down from the tree where he'd been hiding. He quickly unhinged the cage door and let Mrs Pepperpot out. Then he hopped in himself and Mrs Pepperpot shut the door behind him.

'Well done!' he said. 'I watched the whole performance and you certainly gave that old cat just the right medicine.'

Mrs Pepperpot was still shaking with anger. 'She won't be wanting to borrow from me again in a hurry! Of all the ungrateful, two-faced . . .' But Mrs Pepperpot didn't have time to finish her sentence because just then she grew to her normal size. She picked up the cage with Suchislife inside and knocked on the front door.

Inside there was so much noise going on that they

didn't hear Mrs Pepperpot's knock, so she walked in.

What a sight! Mrs Happy was lying on the sofa, moaning and holding her head, while two of her guests were mopping up the third who had had the whole pot of tea spilt over her! They didn't seem to see Mrs Pepperpot, so she put the cage on the table and said: 'I found this in the garden. I suppose it must be the bird you were telling me about, the one that talks so well?'

'Take it away, Mrs Pepperpot, take it away!' groaned Mrs Happy. 'I never want to see it again!'

'But I thought it was the cleverest bird alive,' said Mrs Pepperpot, who could hardly keep from smiling.

'It's far too clever for me,' said Mrs Happy, 'and I'd be pleased if you would accept it as a present—in return for all the nice things you've done for me this summer.'

'Don't mention it, Mrs Happy,' said Mrs Pepperpot,

'but I'd be glad to take Suchis life—I mean Pipkins—home, if you really don't want him any more.'

Then Mrs Pepperpot carried the cage out of the door, down the path and through the handsome wrought-iron gates, and the little blue bird just jumped and down inside, saying one word over and over again: 'Happy, happy, happy, happy!'

'I'm happy too,' said Mrs Pepperpot.